T1-BIQ-578

SACRAMENTO PUBLIC LIBRARY
3 3029 05793 4689

Star Climbing

by Lou Fancher

paintings by Steve Johnson and Lou Fancher

Laura Geringer Books
An Imprint of HarperCollins*Publishers*

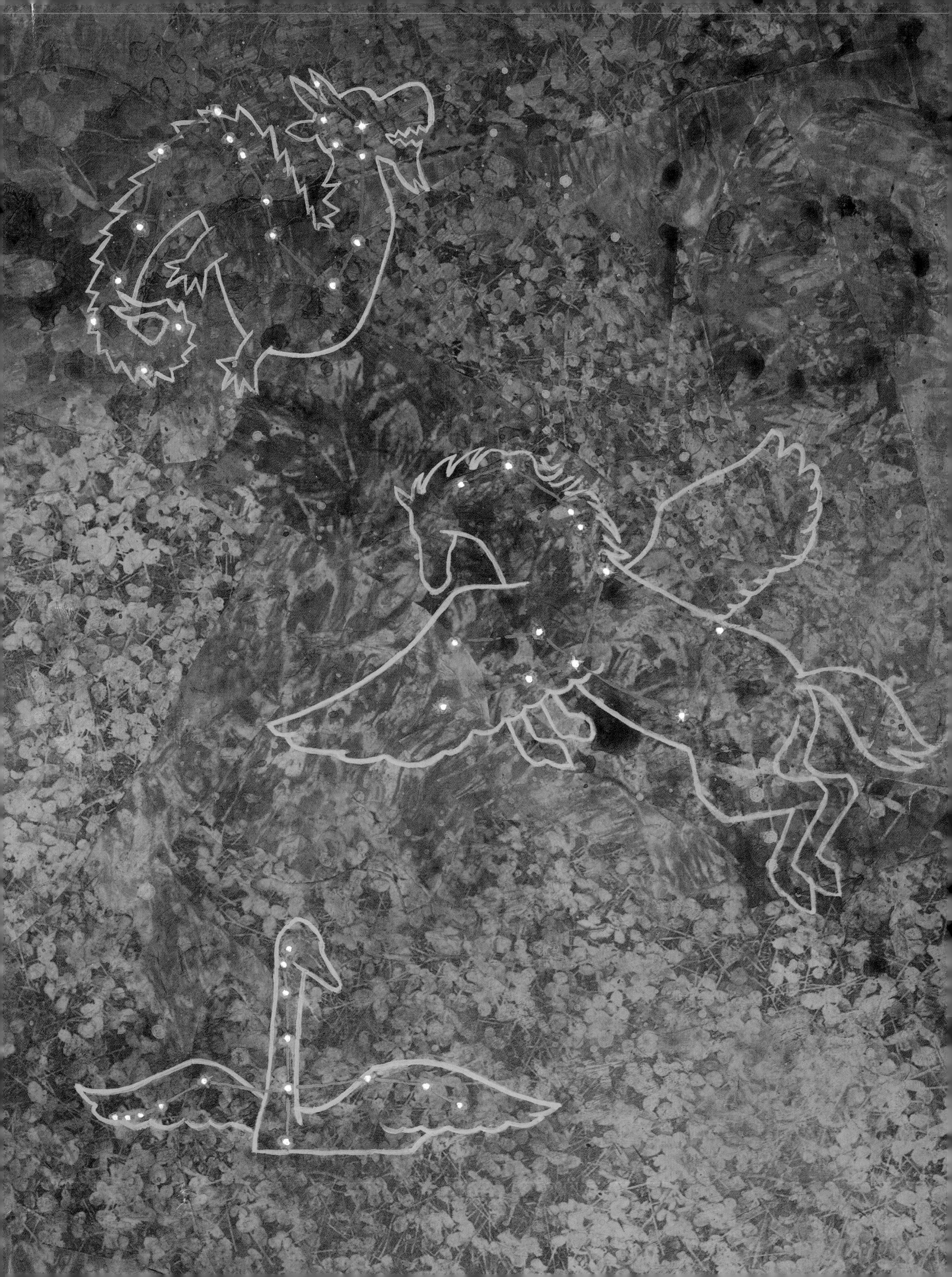

On nights I cannot sleep,
I go star climbing.

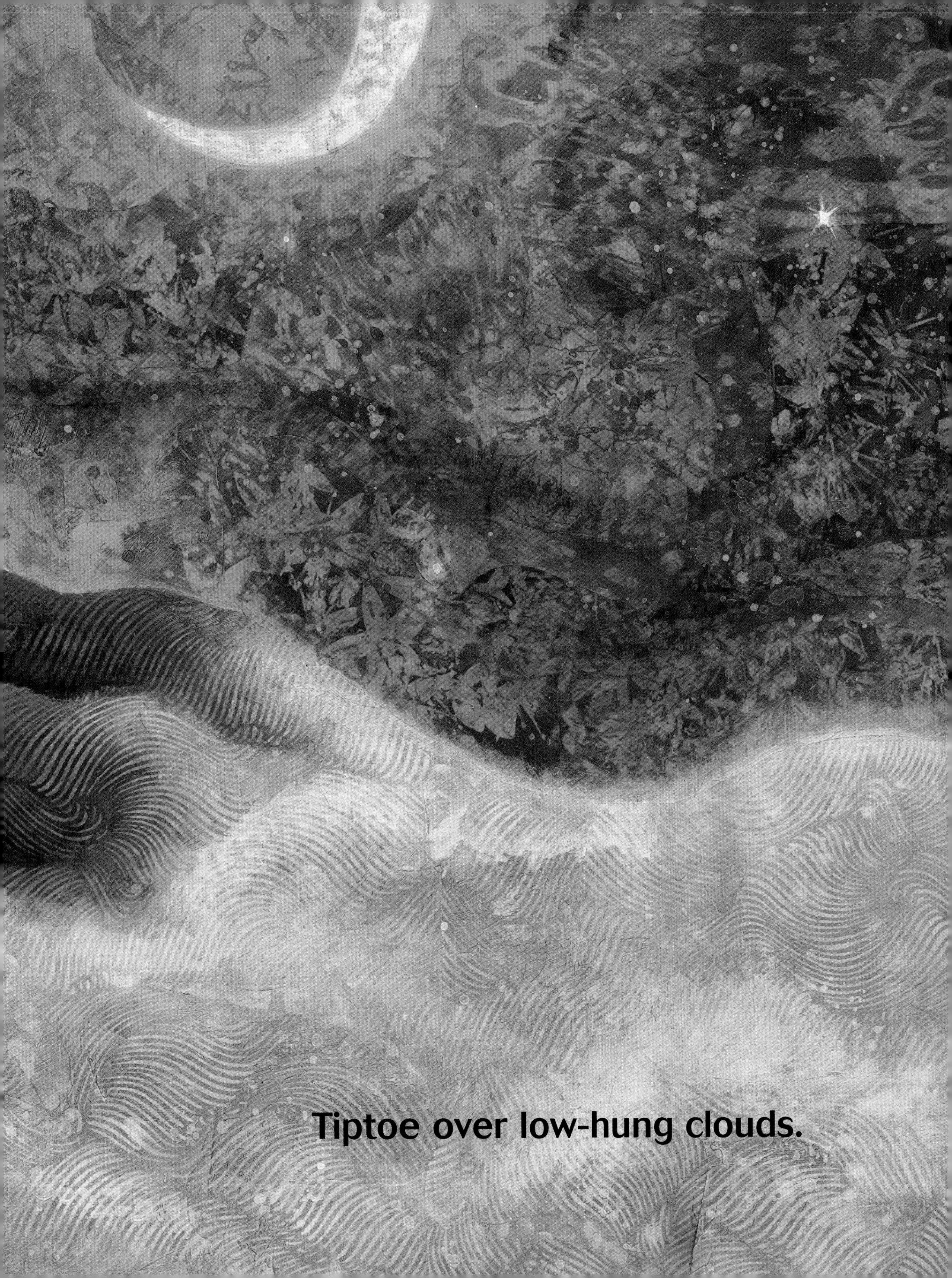

Tiptoe over low-hung clouds.

Leap from star to shining star.

Skip across
bright silver
stones.

Dive into a
golden pool.

Toss a star through black of night.

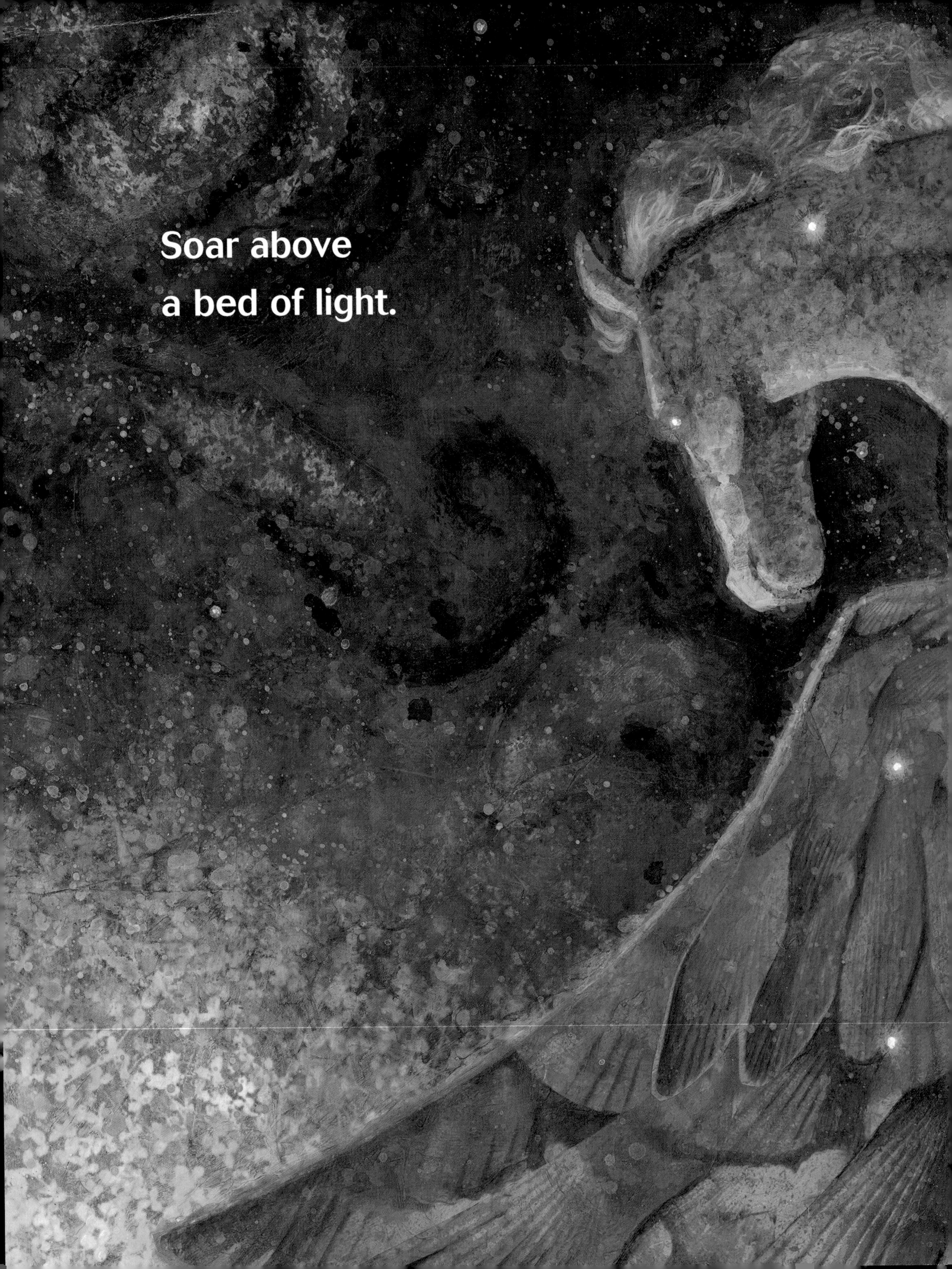

Soar above
a bed of light.

Float across the

blue-hush sky.

Eyelids heavy,
gently closing,

Drift and dream past tender moon.

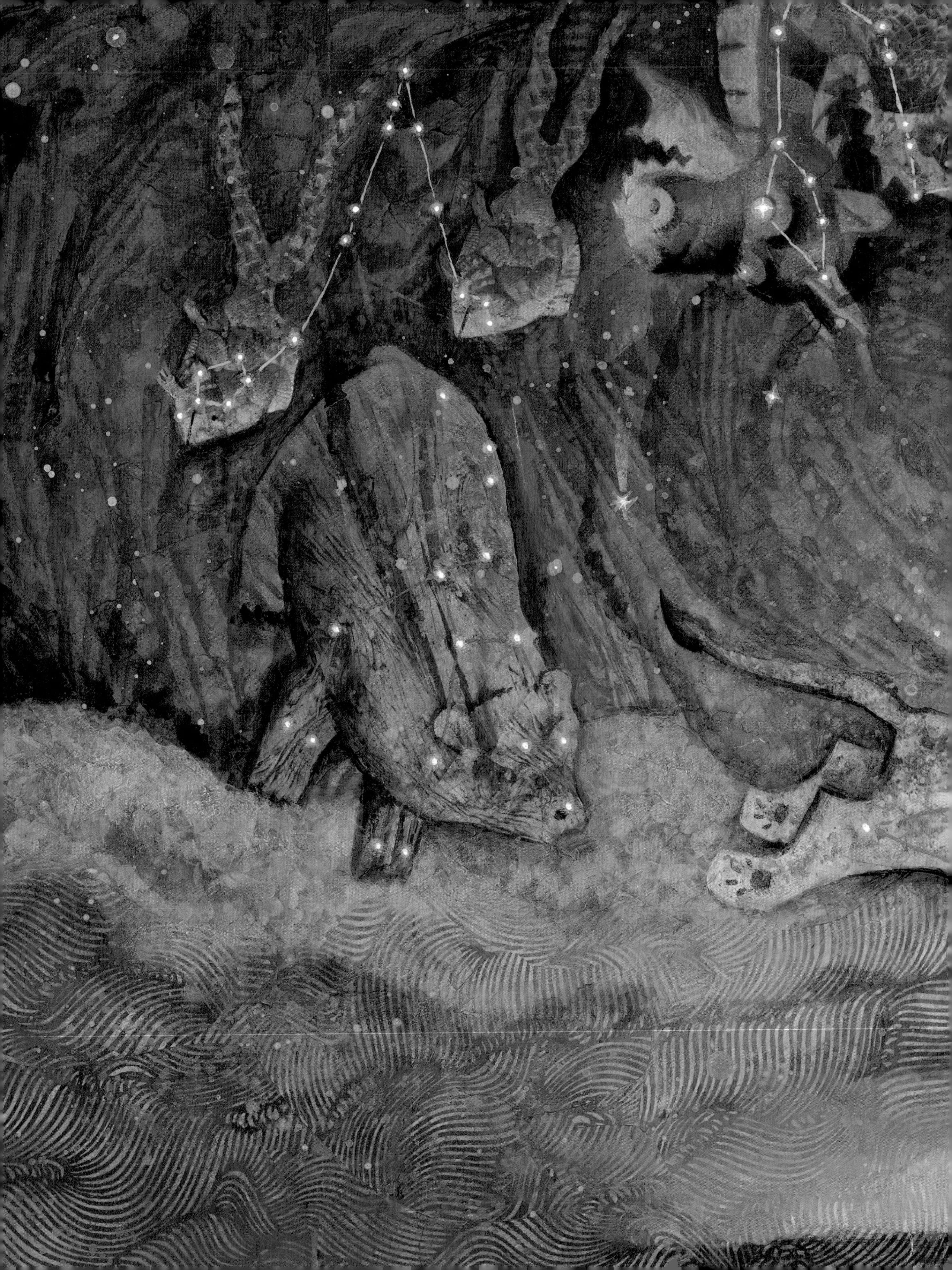

Leaving clouds and night behind,
Mother Star begins to rise.

Tucked and curled and warm, I wake

To glowing sun . . . and day . . . and home.

In ancient times, people saw heroes, creatures, and objects in the stars. Civilizations all over the earth told legends and myths about these shining images. Today, astronomers divide the sky into regions, called constellations, often naming the areas after the original shapes seen in the night sky.

Leo (the Lion): With skin so tough that arrows could not pierce his hide, the lion fell under the bold hands of Hercules, the strongest of all of Zeus's sons, and was immortalized in the sky.

Ursa Major (the Great Bear): The huntress Callisto was turned into a bear by Zeus's jealous wife, Hera. To prevent Callisto's son, Arcas, also a hunter, from accidentally killing his own mother, Zeus turned Arcas into Little Bear and cast them both into the sky.

Pisces (the Fish): To escape the many-headed monster Typhon, Aphrodite, the Greek goddess of love, and her son, Eros, turned themselves into fish and swam to safety.

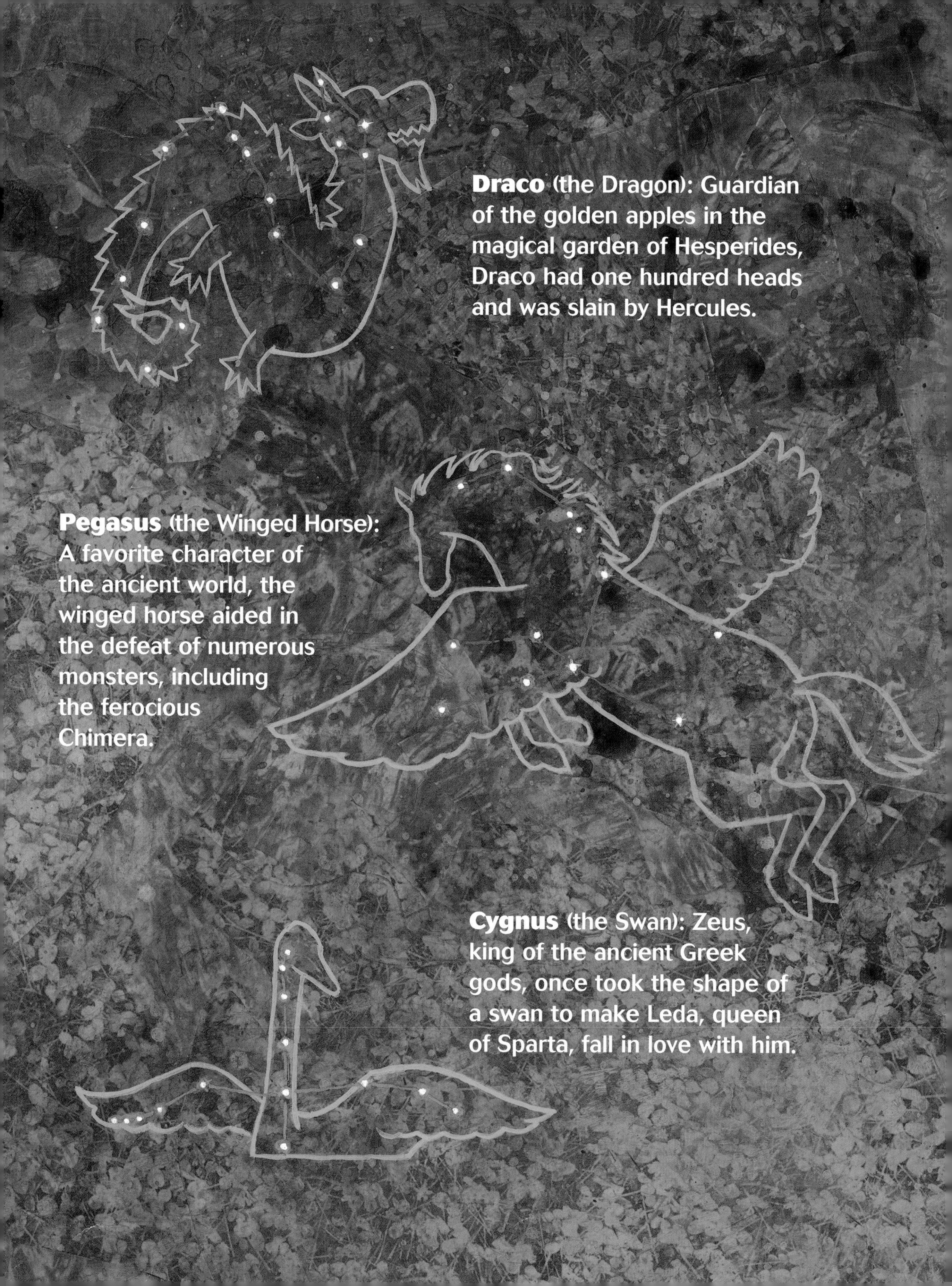

Draco (the Dragon): Guardian of the golden apples in the magical garden of Hesperides, Draco had one hundred heads and was slain by Hercules.

Pegasus (the Winged Horse): A favorite character of the ancient world, the winged horse aided in the defeat of numerous monsters, including the ferocious Chimera.

Cygnus (the Swan): Zeus, king of the ancient Greek gods, once took the shape of a swan to make Leda, queen of Sparta, fall in love with him.

For Ann

—L.F.

Star Climbing

Manufactured in China by South China Printing Company Ltd.
 For information address HarperCollins Children's Books, a division of HarperCollins Publishers, 1350 Avenue of the Americas, New York, NY 10019.
www.harperchildrens.com

Library of Congress Cataloging-in-Publication Data
Fancher, Lou.
Star climbing / by Lou Fancher ; illustrated by Steve Johnson and Lou Fancher.— 1st ed.
p. cm.
Summary: When he cannot sleep, a little boy imagines himself on a nighttime journey across the sky where he can run and dance with star constellations.
ISBN-10: 0-06-073901-0 — ISBN-10: 0-06-073902-9 (lib. bdg.)
ISBN-13: 978-0-06-073901-0 — ISBN-13: 978-0-06-073902-7 (lib. bdg.)
[1. Stars—Fiction. 2. Constellations—Fiction. 3. Imagination—Fiction. 4. Bedtime—Fiction.] I. Johnson, Steve, date, ill. II. Title.
PZ7.F1988Sta 2006
[E]—dc22
2005005048
CIP
AC

Design by Lou Fancher
1 2 3 4 5 6 7 8 9 10
❖
First Edition